The Adventures of Bella and Lily
The Beginning

Stephanie Pulaski

AuthorHouse™
1663 Liberty Drive
Bloomington, IN 47403
www.authorhouse.com
Phone: 1 (800) 839-8640

Published by AuthorHouse 09/14/2018

ISBN: 978-1-5462-5886-5 (sc)
978-1-5462-5885-8 (e)

Library of Congress Control Number: 2018910895

Print information available on the last page.

authorHOUSE®

DEDICATION

Jacob thank you for keeping the dream alive, believing in me and the 1,001 reads.

Dad and Mom thank you for the amazing blessing and prayers.

Our beautiful daughter Izzy, I hope this book shows you that you really can do anything in life with family, support and God's love.

Bella, Belly, Tiger, Big Girl, Bella Simone-rice a roney you will always be the best dog anyone could ask for.

Hi, my name is Bella Simon Pulaski, and I am going to share my adventures with you. I want to start my first adventure in sunny California at the local pound.

I was adopted at the pound by my new mommy and daddy. I was so happy to go home with them! My daddy nicknamed me "big girl" because when I am happy I shake my little tail. Mommy nicknamed me "Tiger" because of my stripes.

When I got to my new home I was so happy. There was a nice big bed just for me. I even had toys to play with. I also get to go on car rides and walks. Sometimes I even get drive-thru French fries. I love my new family.

The weekends are the best, because we get to go places together as a family. The beach is my favorite place to go, the water is cold and you never know what friends you will meet.

Today is going to be a great day. I get to go to work with my dad. My dad is a Marine that means he serves in the Military. I love getting to see where my dad works and meet his friends, and seeing all the big trucks.

Today is Thanksgiving! I am not sure what that is, but I know it smells good. Mom and Dad have been in the kitchen cooking all day. Some of dad's Marine friends are coming over. I can't wait to try a little of everything and watch some football, or eat a football, maybe both.

I have some more exciting news mom and dad said their families are coming to see us. I hope they know I like to chew on bones. I loved getting to meet my new family members. They took me on walks and taxi rides. I even got French fries! Family is the best and my dad and mom's family truly is. I love them all.

My first year with my family has been amazing. We have already done so much together. But we are about to have another adventure. Dad came home with good news. He told mom we get to move to Texas. They were both really excited; you see that's where my mom and dad are from. I can't wait to go to Texas! I hope I get to take my chew bones with me.

The trip to Texas is so beautiful, I am seeing mountains, deserts, cacti and something called a road runner. He was interesting. Texas at last! I love my new home here, I have a big yard to run and play in. Texas reminds me of California, it's nice and sunny here. It's fun to chase dragonflies, too.

I love getting to take walks in the neighborhood. I am meeting so many new friends; some were even from the pound like me. Being adopted by an awesome family who truly loves me is the best thing any dog could ask for.

Mom and Dad told me they have some exciting news to tell me. I think it's going to be another adventure...

Printed in the United States
By Bookmasters